MISTS OF MYSTERIES

AASHI CHAUHAN

Contents

Foreword

As children, we all envision ourselves as protagonists of our own thriller stories: the 007s and Sawyers of our lives, and it is the moral responsibility of all authors, all across the globe, to continue to add timber to this flame of imagination, bit by bit, that the flame may stay ever bright.

For many, this imagination is the driving force - the Kaizen - that sustains them through the exasperation and monotony that is an unfortunate by-product of quotidian life. For others, it is a simple means of entertainment.

But for most, it is simply a necessity.

In this fashion, an author is not much different from a relief worker or a doctor.

So, as you flip this page and take your first steps towards unravelling the mystery that underlies the pieces of paper, my only suggestion to you is this: do not be afraid to imagine, hope, and theorise.

For a mystery story has multiple branches to it: one that the writer chooses to unravel; others that the readers must uncover themselves.

Preface

What if a murderer gets murdered, except the murder was not a murder?

A bizarre tongue twister to base a story around.

I guess it all began with two films (that I cannot name for...legal reasons). Films that acquainted me to the mysterious nature of the world. The Bermuda Triangle. The death of Hitler. Mount Kailash. The list goes on...

Thus came about this idea: bringing a tinge of this mystery to you, through the story of Althea. This craving for mystery drove everything from the name of the protagonist to the setting.

If you enjoy reading this story even a fraction as much as I enjoyed writing...

...I'll consider I've done a good job.

- Your author

Acknowledgements

As an endeavouring 'debutante' in the field of authors, publishing this book would have, perhaps, been an unthinkable and impossible feat, if not for the tremendous and unwavering support I garnered and received over the course of my journey.

I am, and will be, perennially grateful to...

...my parents—mom and dad, whose constant encouragement gave me inspiration that kindled the flames of both my curiosity and creativity...

...my Folks—ever-so-important friends, my lifelines...my loves

...and, specially, all of you—readers who are the sole reason why I find it rewarding to spend time weaving words...

...for no book, if it is to be a work of art, can be written through the devotion of a single person.

ONE

THE MAN WANTS TO KILL YOU

This is a story about the man who wants to kill you. I've my dubieties, not about the man or about the story, but about you. I sweat I do all this for nothing. Hear I would scream if I had a mouth. I've a story. So that's what I'll use. You have seen him ahead. He might as well live in your fringe. He's altitudinous and seems to carry his weight in his casket and shoulders. He has a narrow midriff and legs that taper down to small leather shoes. Not that you've noticed any of this ahead. You've been detracted, have not you? If I told you this same man walked by your home every day, broke to peer into your window, you wouldn't want to believe me. But you could not say for certain that I am wrong. I am not wrong. He might be veritably near right now. He might indeed be in your house. After all, there are so numerous excellent caching places, are not there? The reverse of a closet, behind the shower curtain, inside a press … . But I am getting ahead of myself. I promised you a story. And maybe we still have time for it. Understand This man isn't from your time. Extra me your unbelief. There are effects beyond your appreciation. You're too old to suppose you know the macrocosm. Twenty times from now, this man lives on the seacoast with his five- time-old son. Their house, a patchwork creation of driftwood and corrugated essence, clings to the side of a rocky precipice. When the drift crashes in, the swab spray splashes against the windows. The sky is the color of sword, and the water is froth- blotched black. Everything is cold, harsh, and wet — except for inside the house.

Warm unheroic light spills out from a window, and a steady cutlet of bank ringlets over from a slanted flue. Inside, the man reads to his son. He sits in a faded orange armchair by the fire, and she lays on her stomach in front of him, interspersing her focus on the dears and the runners turning in her father's hands. "When you finish this story, can you read another?" . He makes a show of looking at half the book that is still remaining and also looking back at her." Formerly tired of this bone?" She shakes her head."No, I just do not want this one to be over. I do not want them to ever end." He smiles and agrees, indeed though he knows she will be asleep long before he will have to pick out a new book. He knows how she feels.

He does not want any of this to be over. He wants to hold onto every alternate, close his fritters around them and keep them safe, keep them from marching on. And it's at that moment that everything goes white — a blast of bedazzling light that disintegrates the scene into dust — and also fades. When the man comes to, he's rammed into the precipice's face, soaked, hanging a many bases above the swells. Above him, the remains of his house a couple dumpy rustic shafts and one reattached orange branch of his armchair. Below him, inky black ocean. His son is gone. He'll search for her for a long, long time. What he eventually finds isn't what he's looking for. He discovers a way to go back. But invention is noway as neat as any of us would like. He can only travel back a set number of times, way before his son is born. So before he goes back, he does his schoolwork. He researches. He spends hours in the libraries of war galleries, flipping through lines, searching for someone new. Searching for you. And also he makes the vault, jumps back a many decades, emerges the same, if a little squeamish for a spell, into a world converted. The colors feel brighter then, the grins wider, flashing ferociously, the eyes emptier and peckish. But of course that is what he'd see. Him, an busybody. Then, a stalwart old world. On his third day back, he finds you, speaks to you. He asks you for the time. His hands are pulsing; his eyes noway leave yours. Do you remember? It was a time or so agone. Your paths keep crossing, but he gets more conservative, becomes a fluttering shadow, in and out of the corners of your life.

Staying. Watching. So where is he now?

Soon you might know better than me. He's tensing his resoluteness now, like a mesh. Hear You killed this man's son. Not yet, not now. Twenty times in the future. Will it make you feel more if I say it was for a " cause"? Or for the " lesser good"? It's true. At least it's true that you 'll tell yourself that when the time comes. I understand you aren't a killer. Neither is this man with the wide shoulders and bitsy shoes who may be in your house right now. But the times change us. Stories change us. You'll be guarding your family, your musketeers, when you shoot losers across the ocean. And he thinks, by killing you, he 'll be redressing the memory of his son. Perhaps you still do n't believe me. But suppose Is there a limit to what you would do for love? Is any price too high to pay? You'll have an answer for that soon, in the trying times ahead, whether you can face it now or not.

You two are veritably analogous. Do you find that intriguing? Applicable? Maybe not. You both love words and tales and the drama, riddle, and madness of being alive. See His story is incompletely your story, too. But no further of this. I sweat it may be too late, and I 've done all I can. Please, hear. Not to me. A sound. Can you hear it? It's inside your home. Perhaps the creak of a door or a soft muffled step on the carpet. Or a shallow inhale of breath that's not yours. He's there, right now. Don't run. Don't call for help. Remember the story. He does n't want this one to end, not like this — and not deep down, not where it counts. Do you? The shadow in the corner. It's not a shadow.

Okay. Your move.

TWO

A TOWN AMIDST

From the ocean, the city would get a hefty force of fish and seaweed, as well as strips of torn rope and lists, instruments, dolls, painted bottles, and indeed essence shafts. Occasionally the drift graced the seacoast with a book, putatively dry and in decent condition.

Other times, the waters would extend in white ringlets and reveal a glass eye, dead armored cranks, or swab- caked teeth. But out of all the mystifications, the lost and arbitrary effects brought onto the reinforcement, the most bountiful and unabating was by far the dead bodies. That's how it started for everyone. Some of us had arrived on boats, in small figures, generally two or three. The lonely corses of those dragged onto the seacoast were frequently left to lounge in the morning sun like driftwood, drying. There's no clearing past the horizon. The sky, no matter how blue, gradated into an opaque nebula, a thick mist. " But what's out there?" I formerly curiously asked the city's chief, a altitudinous man with broad shoulders and spectacles with similar thin frames that his lens sounded to be floating in front of his face. He took his hand to his chin.

" Do you really want to know?" " I do. Tell me, please." " Well, the world, of course," he answered, screaming. · The children played a game as soon as they heard the chime of the city's bell palace. They would speed past the cobblestone thoroughfares, past the city's forecourt, through a narrow path that led directly to the sand. Before a boat arrived, they would scrap and kvetch like geese, placing bets on how numerous dead bodies would end up being recaptured. " Four," one boy yelled. " No, three," another jumped in. The townspeople would head to the beach, wagering small or precious particulars between one another in hushed tones. " Six," a boy cried. " I go there'll be six dead bodies." " Do n't be stupid," an aged man replied.

" A small vessel could noway fit half-a-dozen corses." The swells grew, layering one over another in a series of ruffles. They hit the reinforcement, extending their reach and licking the toes of those bordering to the seacoast. The water ran jitters past my knees, the vessel eventually approached, the bow kissed the beach sluggishly. The children dashed, cutting past the crowd of people, clapping and howling with gaiety. The first to arrive placed their hands on the ledge, also they hunkered their bodies forward, nearly falling into the boat. " There's nothing!" " What?" some people said. " There's nothing then," the boy returned. " The boat's empty." · All the bodies arrived else. Some had no eyes or hair, and their faces sounded overwashed, nearly as if their expressions could melt clean from their skin. Others frequently arrived mangled, with holes and injuries and rotted injuries, as if the weight of the world had twisted and crushed them like paper. The first cadaver I saw right after my appearance was that of a youthful girl. Her mouth was open and bore no teeth, her skin sallow, and her legs so tense, so thin, that if pulled would snap in two like a wishbone. " What do we do with her?" I asked the city's chief. He let his eyes trace the crowd of people around him. The beginners, the people that had arrived with me, listed and turned their heads, lacking understanding. " Well, we bury her, of course," he answered with similar legerity. " Put her under the earth, under the white beach like a seed." The new advents and I watched the townspeople dig a deep gutter, a burial down from the water, down from the ocean's grip. The dead girl laid on the reinforcement while the boat was swept down by the ocean. The sun began to settle behind the mist. " Accelerate," the principal ordered, " before the high drift comes in." We all pitched in to help, sculpturing an ample grave, important lengthier than the girl's body.

" Did it really need to be this big?" I wondered. " Of course," someone answered, " the bigger the hole, the sounder the sleep." We carried her gently, both hands on her body as if she was a precious doll drafted out of thin demitasse. I helped the townsfolk place her into the earth and watched them cover her with beach like a time capsule. " What do we do now?" I asked. " We stay," said the chief. " For what?" He looked at me, smiled. " Did n't you pay attention?" he asked. " The youthful girl's been buried, so now we 'll stay for her to rise and live; so that one day she may leave." · When no bodies arrived, but a boat rolled by, it meant that someone's time had come and that they should go. " Go where? Where do they've to go?" " Did n't I formerly tell you, boy?" the principal returned. " Do n't you formerly know what's past the mist?" " You said it was the world." " That's right!" " But is n't this place part of the world too? I do n't get it?" " This place, this city is n't meant for the living."

I had n't discovered at the time what was out towards the direction of the world; everyone who had ever left had yet to ever return. · Out on the other side of the seacoast, abandoned in an area with jagged gemstone conformations as sharp as mountain peaks, was a large vessel with cruises and poles and crooked faces etched into the woodwork. The boat fluently could have transported several hundred people, men, women with children, and clusters of creatures. The swells broke over its housing, expiring a howl analogous to the trees. " So there you are," I heard the principal cry from behind me. " I 've been looking for you." " For me? Why?" " It's my job to ask you, as this city's selectman, if you want to leave." " What do you mean?" I returned. " I ca n't leave; I 'm just a sprat." " But you ca n't stay then much longer moreover." " Why not?" " Like you 've heard me say before this city isn't meant for the living." The principal scrunched down beside me, letting out a moan as if he was weak in the knees. Still," he said, " you can stay, " If you want." " Really!?" " Of course, but if you stay, you can noway leave." " But what's the problem with that?" The chief refocused over my head to the waters of the ocean behind me. " The problem is that you 'll leave the world before, everything you 've come to know, and anything still to be discovered."

The horizon for a moment appeared nearly visible, gauzy indeed. The mass body of the nebulous sub caste hulled down like soft cotton, just enough for me to see the blue sky on the other side with clarity. " Have you had any dreams?" the principal asked. I jounced. " I 've seen people. People, I do n't know, that I do n't remember, swarming around me, stroking my impertinence, bruiting in my observance." " Anything differently?" " Bedazzling lights, two rings, speeding towards me." " And when you wake, what do you feel?" . " In the morning, it felt like a weight on my casket. It was as if my heart was being squeezed and could burst at any moment and stop beating." " And now?" " Now?" I repeated. " Now, I have n't noticed anything." · I sat on the boat with two other people, a man with hair that looked like a pile of crows feathers and the girl that arrived on the seacoast with skinny legs and no teeth, not too long after me. " Are you guys spooked?" she asked. " No, I 'm sure we 'll be fine," he answered with a warm tone. " After all, if we do end up dying before making it past the mist, would n't we just be dragged back to the seacoast?" . The girl laughed, " I guess that's true, is n't it? And what about you, are you upset?" . " I 'm … I 'm spooked," I choked out. " Of what?" she asked. " Of the world, of what's past the mist." " Do n't be," she assured, putting her hand on my stage. " You have to believe that the world's worth seeing." · The boat rocked, causing our bodies to shift forward and back, following the sway of the ocean. The water rumored and splashed against the housing, percolating a salty scent while transferring driblets into the air that stuck to our skin. " The mist," the man with the feathered hair let out. He gestured with his head to the shape- shifting shadows boxing our vessel. " It's thick," I remarked, squinting. But no bone answered. The man and the girl were gone, their bodies absorbed by the mist. I had no idea what was going on. I ran to the end of the boat, nearly tripping and falling into the water.

The overlay was eating the wood down, painting everything in my vicinity in white panorama. Everything entwined the townspeople, the sand, the chief, the jarring kiddies. The sound of swells crashing, the dead, the weight of the beach over my buried body, the townspeople gathering around me. I looked out to where the city should have been and reminded myself of the chief's words. I was swept by a surge of idle recollections a canine, a house with vines draping from the roof, a man with white hairs, and a woman wearing a sunbonnet, sitting on the stairs of a frontal veranda. There was a youthful girl, important youngish than me, my family, running towards the road. I saw a brace of eyes blinking, bursting into halos, warping the space around me. I heard crying and felt a burning cold marshland over my body. There was a haul, the pull of an unnoticeable hook latched onto my casket.

I felt no pain, and for a moment, it felt as if I were a pall, distancing myself from the dead ocean. In the end, I was suitable to make it back to the world. In the end, I 'm then, living.

THREE

DESTINATION ZERO

I arrived for my flight well ahead of schedule. I knew the time frame and where I demanded to be at this moment. Always being an early raspberry has proven itself to guide me more times than not. When you are on the go, 24-7, you just follow the rule book. By that I mean, get your act together and do not condemn anyone but yourself for your lack of time operation.

Too numerous people aren't on the ball and surely playing on the wrong court. I had my eye on the timepiece, per usual, walking casually on my way, across and into the field hallway. I had my ticket in hand and tried to cross over to the escalator, and also over, over and into the security line. When I had to go where the wind took me for work or rest, I noway played the game we played as kiddies, red light-green light. I learned better not to accelerate up and stay and to always be prepared. Although occasionally you do all the right effects, but also there is that glitch in the matrix when you had not prepared for someone differently taking a wrong turn into your lane. It was only a many twinkles agone, that someone sounded to be having a wild and crazy day and pulled me into it.

The scene was a little over the top, but it only made me shake my head and laugh at the whole incident as I calmly readjusted myself and headed up the escalator. What started off to be just an average day for me changed in a alternate. On the way across the lobby to head upstairs, this big joe came storming into the field entrance of the structure, shoved me out of the way as we crossed paths both heading in contrary directions. He said' sorry'but wasn't sorry as he was on his phone and with his big frame stepped exactly on my bottom. It was each about him. I mugged and swore under my breath but did not let him get the better of me. After taking a deep breath, I progressed within my own trip routine but saw this character large and in charge in the distance thunder down towards another airline ticket counter. And I do mean thunder. His heavy-footed run with the most ginormous bag was ridiculous not just to me but others who he bombarded over in his destination hunt.

He cried at everyone to move out of the way holding his hand out to push down any and every bone that delayed his race to the finish line. I progressed along my jocular way as the delay time in line wasn't an issue and got through security with no detention. There was always a friendly and accommodating staff at this field that made trip for me a breath. Moment, still, I sounded to notice a unforeseen collaboration of advanced ups as several administrators and the field security director talked amongst themselves sometimes pointing one way also another. I am sure it was nothing grand. Just a day in the life of trippers with security help going about their shift duties in a small field. Or so I allowed. I had stepped away to the closest seating area to gather my particulars together and noticed Mister' Large and in Charge' talking out loud to whomever would hear as he awaited in the line of three people to get through security. When he began barking orders to accelerate his delay time, the staff felt it was time to address his rude geste. With a stern, yet calm station the administrator spoke to the big joe who after stating his communication, instantly told him to go to hell.

This contravention sounded to rise to a certain position of interest when shortly after several police officers appeared and independently stood near. They observed the situation and what was going on yet abstain from approaching, more likely waiting, to companion the big joe to his gate without farther ado. I noticed further people came terrified as he now spoke loudly to the officers right to their faces claiming his civil liberties were being put in jeopardy and he'd not be quiet. Was this a ruse? I was done with harkening further to the loudmouth and demanded to leave the situation at the check point. Did he just wink at me? I seized my bag and with nausea, turned and began to walk towards my gate. I couldn't and would not let him ruin my day. The commotion was still heard far down and had yet to lessen. Others noticed but by now sounded to not watch. I had a feeling as I continued to walk that someone differently deliberately began to follow along side. " So, what'd ya suppose ofol' Humpty Dumpty?"I was caught a little off guard but knew exactly what and who she was pertaining to. She was in a different livery than the others but a security staff member for sure. Why she spoke candidly to me was a question of surprise. I answered without vacillation to offer her my foursquare opinion and told her that he was noticed from the get- go as soon as he stepped into the structure.

His ignorant station wasn't the usual style of a stressed-out rubberneck that I had come to observe over the times as he swept through the lobby charging in a bull- fighting manner on his way to the ticket counter. It was egregious that everyone noticed his bad teste. But like any seasoned rubberneck, they, like I, just enough much ignored this lump. We talked further about life in the fast lane, and she was polite in asking about my forthcoming trip and work. It morphed into other places that I'd traveled but fell back into this current situation and how it must be a real challenge for everyone working then right now. She smiled and thanked me for the information. What wasn't added was that the incident would be given a positive check mark and taken to a advanced position for evaluation. We stood at the gate and turned to see what was passing upon hearing quite a loud, but familiar voice approaching from the other end of the field where I had checked in. Several police officers and the bones at the security check point were now convoying. Humpty Dumpty down and out. Supposedly, effects got out of hand as he was now in hand bond. His mow sounded to have noway left his face and he continued to spew angry words scolding one and all. He glanced over with a boo, and I wanted to shove him so hard but defied when the officers forcefully took him out and into the team auto.

" Good! "she replied in hearing his raving badinage vanish into the business and knowing her job was over for the day. "He went over easy. Sunnyside down.

FOUR

THE DISAPPEARING GONG

I've lost numerous effects in my life, but the ding my mama gave me sticks out in my mind the most. Its sound. Warming it up. The crash. Like a storm on a cuisine visage blasting toward Heaven. Over time, I lost it in a move or commodity at some point. I 'm not exactly sure when or where. I used to suppose about it every night before I fell asleep. I suppose about everything I 've ever lost. They all kill me. They all feel like a piece of my history that I'll noway recoup, and they always end on the gong. Losing it felt like I had lost a part of my mama.

Although people pass down, the particulars they leave before are lucky enough to continue living for them. Its climate would feel like, for a moment, her ghost was physically in the room with me. I missed it so intensively. Until a many days agone, when by chance, I plant it again. Walking the two blocks toward my favorite coffee shop, as I do utmost mornings, I passed a neighbor hosting a small yard trade on the patch of lawn in front of her home. Anyhow of being raised in Chicago and living then my entire life, I ever still knew veritably little about the people around me. In her mound of old DVDs, coliseums, and normal cabinetwork, it sat on top of a bookshelf and shined brightly in the morning sun. My gong. It had to be the same bone. The perfect dimples on its golden face. One large blue circle was painted around the external edge, with a lower, lighter blue circle running around outside. A red string handle was attached on top. I've no way seen another like it.

Of course, to be sure, I demanded to hear its crash. " Hi," she said, putting down her book and leaning forward in her folding president, smiling at me, " Got your eye on that gong?" . Her eyes were kind, and her blarney shirt was calming. She had no idea that this thing used to belong to me. There was no malignancy in her suggestion. She had simply seen my interest and wanted to know if she could make me happy. She presumably would have just given it to me. " I was wondering if I could strike it. You know, to see how it sounds," I said. " Of course. The mallet is nearly hard. It should be over there. You know a lot about gongs?" The smooth beach- colored rustic mallet was sitting in a pile of dirt beside the bookshelf. The neglectfulness of this arrangement made my blood pustule. They didn't earn this gong. I seized the mallet, dusted it off, held the godly cymbal in front of my casket, and began to warm up a crash. A shiver of the great top approaching washed over me as I was transported to the frontal row of an angelic band playing the notes of rain. Volcanos erupted. My entire life melted down my eyelids, and I noway wanted to open them or see anything again. I wanted to live in this sound. I was reunited with that old friend that I so foolishly lost. It was mine again.

" I 'll take this," I said, holding it up advanced as if she did n't formerly know what I meant. " I 'm glad you like it. One of my son's fellows brought it over one time and left it then. Also she left it then when she went to council this time and wo n't text me back when I ask if she wants it, so I told her that I was going to vend it or contribute it, and she still did n't respond. Kiddies." " That's great. How important is it?" " Oh, I do n't know. You feel like the expert. How much does a gong go for?" " It's priceless." " How's twenty bucks sound? You feel like you like it. I 'm happy to see that indeed if I take a beating on the price." As I produced the plutocrat from my fund, another man approached our meeting. He was shorter than me and wearing dark apparel. His hair was thinning, and a medical mask obscured his face. He'd been lurking around, pretending to look at particulars. Once he saw that I was about to buy the gong, he interposed. " I believe that item is mine," he stammered. " Sorry confidante, he beat you to it," the woman said. " This same gong was stolen from me a long time agone. I lost stopgap that I would ever see it or hear it again. That's until I heard this man strike it. I 'm certain it's my stolen gong." He approached me and reached out a hand to touch the gong. I pulled it down.

" I 'm sorry to hear about your loss, joe," I said, " but I 'm sure there are numerous gongs that look like this. You ca n't be certain it's yours." " I'm certain," he said, " I supplicate your amnesty, but please return my property." " I do n't know where my son's swain got this thing, but I misdoubt he stole it from you. That would be weird as hell. I 'm sure this is a misreading. This man was then first. He gets to the buy the gong. That's it." She seized the plutocrat out of my hand and jounced at me. The man listed his head forward and looked up at me through swinging beaches of what slithery hair he still had left. I ran back to my apartment, fully forgetting about coffee or the day ahead of me. I had my gong back, and I could n't let it out of my sight again. I hung it above the fireplace in my living room. The perfect spot. The look of it. Its implicit energy screamed the sound of its rise and fall in my mind without producing any factual noise. Each time I struck it, my mama's ghost felt like it was in the living room with me for the duration of its fall. The fireplace only amplified this effect. Fire and essence, splashing together in a ocean of emotion that held my entire life in its hands. I felt whole again. I felt like I had reclaimed a piece of my history. It was a alternate chance.

Also, in the middle of the night, I was awakened by a splitting crash. I sprang from my bed and ran out into my living room to see the ding swinging above the fireplace. It had easily been struck, but at least it hadn't been stolen. This sound was different. It didn't bring my mama's spirit. I turned on the lights, but there was no meddler. I searched for hours. My apartment was empty. I called the police, but they were harmful. They looked around and told me there was nothing they could do. Neighbors did n't see anything. One officer said they would record fresh drive-by checks in the area and suggested buying a home security camera. Also they left. The coming night, it happed again. Although I had been trying to stay awake in an trouble to catch the returning malefactor, at around 1 AM, sleep consumed my pulsing heart just before a loud crash rattled my home, and the perceptivity sculpted into my cognizance for that sound started harsh temblors throughout my body. Again, I ran around the apartment in hunt of no bone. I was alone. The police did nothing. I could only sit and suppose about the man from that day at my neighbor's yard trade until the daylight. Of course, I considered going to the woman's house again and asking if she knew anything about him. It did n't feel as though they had met ahead, given theirexchange.However, creating a stronger bond with my neighbors would help me feel safer, If nothing differently. I wanted eyes around the community. Still, when I went to her home the ensuing evening, she was gone. She had moved.

That's why she was having the garage trade. The house was for trade. I laughed at how unobservant I had been. Also I was struck with horror. The ding was sitting in my apartment wholly vulnerable. Maybe the meddler, that man, would return. When I arrived back home, there was no substantiation of a break- heft. My treasure was safely hanging above the fireplace. I decided to take the gong into my room. I would not fall asleep on this night. I put it in my closet. Locked down behind my clothes, facing the bottom of my bed, anyone trying to touch it would have to pass me, and I would be ready. I 'm not exactly sure what time it happed, but as I sat and goggled at the closet door, I sluggishly began to nod out. I do n't remember ever falling asleep, but I do n't know how it could have happed if I did n't because a loud crash from the gong chimed out behind my closet door and rattled its frame. It warmed up, blarneying me further into dreams, and broke my hypnotism upon the crash of its release. I screamed. There was no way someone could have snuck into my closet. Insolvable. I had been watching it the entire evening. I sluggishly stood up from my bed and cautiously approached the door. Once I plucked up enough courage to open it, I plant commodity that shook me to my core. Inside the closet, there was neither an meddler nor a gong. There was nothing. The ding was gone.

I searched the closet for hours. It was gone. It was nowhere. I searched the rest of my apartment. Maybe I moved it in my sleep. There was nothing. It had simply dissolved. The police held back horselaugh as I again reported mischief related to my gong. They assumed it was a friend of mine playing a knavery. They said they would be on the lookout for it but did n't ask for a description. I asked if they wanted to smoke for fingerprints, and they said it would be useless. My gong was gone again, and it would stay gone this time. The meddler, whoever it was, didn't return. Now, when I lie awake at night, I no longer suppose about the effects I 've lost. I believe that they're lost for a reason. I'm not meant to have them back. They're no longer mine.

I no longer dream about the ding's beautiful noise. I sweat it. I supplicate that terrible crash won't ring out again to tease and afflict me. The feeling of missing family and effects had been replaced by crippling anxiety, like awaiting a sneeze that noway comes, staying for that ding's cry. The absence of sound took on a heavier weight. The silence showed itself to be the coming subcaste of Hell to peel down for me to couloir.

Ultimately, I plant comfort in it and smiled. You must enjoy these effects while you can. You'll miss them when they 're gone.

FIVE

PHANTOM OF THE OPERA

The lights shroud and the followership's exchanges dock as they eagerly stay for the play to begin. A loud BANG rings through the extensive theater, and the followership gasps, still, the stage remains dark and black.

The curtains lie motionless, trickling down to the bottom like melting velvet ice cream. The show has not yet begun. That being as it is, also how come a shot chimed through the theater? . Because it wasn't part of the act. The day following, the Sunday Weekly was published, listing details about what passed that day. A shot chimed through the Winston Tabernacle Theater on the night of November 22nd of 1969, killing Herman McKinney, a medical worker at the Clayton Hospital on 24th road. According to Kathrine McKinney, Herman's woman who was sitting beside him when the accident passed, the pellet hit him in the casket, and she knew right down that there was no stopgap. When the ambulance arrived, she appeared to be correct.

The pellet killed him within twinkles, and there was, in fact, no stopgap for the croaker. Officer Andy Smith saw a man fleeing the scene, and incontinently contended after the figure with his mate, George Bennett. They chased the figure down to the corner of Main and 25th Road. Andy and his mate saw the man for the briefest of moments, but they both described him as follows; dark green eyes the color of jungle vines, crimpy chocolate-brown hair, and an oddly shaped scar on his forepart. He was last wearing a dark black fleece with muddy brown thrills. Report this figure incontinently if seen, and report any suspicious geste to the authorities. Police are presently probing the case with a professional. Officer Andy Smith, Officer George Bennett, their commanding officer, and a operative known as Professor Brown all sat in a large chamber. Andy Smith was oriented to working with investigators, but this bone was different. Professor Brown, as the operative was known, gave him an inexpressible feeling. He sounded so familiar, yet he could n't put his cutlet on why. Had they met ahead? He claimed to be following the perpetrator of these violent acts that had been being in other locales throughout the state. The killer would essay to murder someone in a theatre. Attempt. Supposedly, this was the first time the killer had actually succeeded in his violent acts. Professor Brown walked into the office the morning following the incident.

He claimed to know about the case, and also progressed to explain to Andy, George, and their commanding officer each that he knew concerning the " Phantom of the Opera", as the miscreant came given. When Professor Brown was finished explaining his case, he acclimated his chapeau and asked Andy, George, and the principal officer what had passed that night, and that he wished to see substantiation that may lead to the perpetrator. " Officer Smith-" " Please, call me Andy." Andy claimed. " Alright also." The Professor agreed. " Andy, if I'm not incorrect, you were there when this incident happed, correct?" . " Well, yes." Andy replied. " I was there. George and I chased the felonious down to the corner of 25th and Main until we lost him. He ran into the abandoned fix plant on the corner. We followed him in, but he just. Faded." " Hmm." Professor Brown traced off. " Do you have any substantiation that I may examine?" " Indeed we do, joe." The principal officer walked off into another room, and returned with a couple of zip- bloc bags. Inside were pieces of attestation of which the Professor would examine. " We hope these prove useful to your disquisition." " I 'm sure they will," said the Professor. He opened the bag labeled# 1023 77A and gazed outside. He pulled out a bitsy pellet covered in dry blood. " Is this the pellet that killedMr. McKinney?" " Yes," said George. " Because of the blood, we have n't been suitable to match it to any specific person or gun." He walked forward and looked nearly at the pellet. " I tête-àtête suppose the Phantom would have just used a regular dynamo." Professor Brown jounced. "I would agree with that,Mr. Bennett." He gazed at the pellet, nearly squinting his eyes. " Yes indeed. I would also conclude that this pellet was fired by a dynamo."

They all stood there in an creepy silence until the commander said " We should leave you to look over the substantiation. We would n't want to disturb you." Andy, George, and their principal also left the room, leaving Professor Brown alone to work. When the door was completely shut, the commander said to George and Andy to do anything the professor told them. They jounced, and the principal walked off. Andy still could n't find out what it was with Professor Brown. He sounded so strange, so familiar. It was on the tip of his lingo. What was it? " George?" Andy rumored. George looked over, and Andy continued. " Does not the professor feel. Strange to you? Familiar, perhaps?" Andy looked down. " I do n't know. I just have this feeling." " Andy, when has your gut ever been right?" George joked. Andy wanted to laugh, but just could n't. This was serious, but supposedly George did n't suppose so. Andy decided that George was presumably right. When has his gut ever been right? His studies were intruded by Professor Brown opening the door. He walked out carrying a sprinkle of lines, looking like a busy business man. " So you traced the DNA back to these three suspects, correct?" He dug out three papers from his towering mound and projected them to the bulletin board on the wall that was behind the office. Each paper had a picture and a name.

The first read SUZANE JACOBS, and had on it a picture of a 30 or so time old lady with limp orange hair and bright blue eyes the color of clear ocean water. She had on an elegant black chapeau with pure white feathers popping out from the right side. On the alternate paper was the name THOMAS BANKS, and on it was also the picture of a youthful boy who could be no aged than 7, who looked like he still slept in a racecar bed. He'd golden hair that was slightly messy and blue eyes that sounded to bulge oddly out of his head. The final paper had the name LUCY WRIGHT on it, and had the picture of a 20-ish time old woman who wore a fancy black dress. She had brown hair, brown eyes, and had on a graceful choker with a bitsy gem in the center. " Well," responded George. " We did come up with those people, but you left out Winfred Noble and Herman McKinney." He searched the mound of papers for a moment or two before pulling out two wastes of paper that were analogous to the others—a name and a snap. One had the name WINFRED NOBLE and the other HERMAN McKinney. Still, the ultimate, unlike the rest, had the word

Stiff in the corner, as Herman McKinney had passed on. The picture ofMr. Noble was of an aged man, maybe in his late 40's, who had brown hair with grays sprouting up then and there. He'd on a suit and tie, and he'd hazel- colored eyes the color of caramel. " My justifications," spoke the Professor. " I trust that you have spoken with these suspects?" " Indeed we have, joe. None of them had any information concerning the case," said Andy. He also added, " and the little boy was so alarmed, so we did n't ask him numerous questions. He is n't a suspect, but he may have some information we need," . " Would it be possible," the Professor asked, " for me myself to question these people?" Easily Professor Brown was wanting for further information to check. " Well, I suppose so," George said, uncertainly. The Professor jounced. " Okay also, let us go." Andy, George, and Professor Brown tracked down all of the suspects, starting with Thomas Banks.

" Son, could you tell me what happed that night?" The Professor questioned. He shifted his bases nervously. " Well, I was with Mommy and Daddy, and we were going to see a show. The lights got darker and Mommy rumored to me that the show was starting, and everyone got quiet. Also I heard a projectile, and started to cry. Just a bit however. Mommy told me that it was okay and it was just part of the show. I calmed down. There were a many riots and Daddy started to get nervous. I told him it was just part of the show to calm him down, too, but he was still spooked. Also we plant out that someone had actually failed. It's sad." " It's sad," Andy said, looking down. Professor Brown allowed for a moment, also asked " can you tell me where you had been before that?" . Thomas allowed for a moment, also said, " oh! I went to the restroom about.10 twinkles before the show! I got kind of lost, however, and ended up in a weird room with a bunch of chairpersons and tables and stuff like that piled up in heaps." " Intriguing. Thank you, Thomas." The Professor puzzled for a moment and left the room. The others also said kindly the same effects. Lucy Wright said, " I had gotten lost when I was walking into the theater, and wound up in a storehouse room full of cabinetwork boxes." The same was with Suzane Jacobs. " I had lost my reading spectacles right before the play began, and I went to look for them in a storehouse room kind of place, and when I came back, a man had been boggled." Winfred Noble also said some of the same. " I was looking for the bathroom and came misplaced. I, rather, plant a large storehouse room filled with cabinetwork, boxes and other particulars." Andy, George, and the Professor met up in another room to dissect the information. " You have checked the security footage, correct?". " Yes, joe," George responded. " There was nothing there." " Well," said the Professor. " Let us check again!" They took him to the theatre and asked to see the security footage of the storehouse room the suspects had described from the night of the 22nd. As Andy had said, there was nothing but static. " See?" Andy began to walk out. " Stay!" Cried the Professor. " Look at this!" Andy whirled around and saw factual camera footage! " This is insolvable," he muttered, shocked. " We watched the whole footage and there was nothing." He traced off, millions of studies flying through his head.

How is this possible? His questions had no answers. His studies, no conclusions. Professor Brown suggested, " perhaps the cameras were conking, also. Maybe they just demanded time?" It was reasonable, so Andy agreed. They saw Thomas adventure into the room, his face wet with gashes, calling for his parents. Latterly, they sawMrs. Jacobs walk into the room, looking for her spectacles, but she left empty handed. Latterly still, they saw Miss Wright peep in the room and walk around in it for a nanosecond, also leave. Still, they saw no sign of Winfred Noble. " Well done Professor," Andy said. " You 've caught the Phantom of the Opera." The three also walked out of the Winston Tabernacle Theater to report their findings. They had been suitable to admit a hunt leave and knocked on the door of Winfred Noble. They searched his house and plant indeed more substantiation. Andy paraded over to Professor Brown. " You know," he said. " I had my dubieties about you, but you have truly proven yourself. Good job, Professor." And he meant every word. "Mr. Noble," Professor Brown questioned. " Is it true that you were out of city on the 3 rd of October just last month?" " Yes, joe," Winfred replied. " I was visiting family." " Where did you travel to?" The Professor asked. " I went to Pineville, West Virginia." " Intriguing," the Professor went on. " Because that's exactly where another murder was tried!" Winfred's countenance was full of shock. His eyes incontinently grew twice their size. He was alarmed. " No! It was n't me!" " Then!" Cried another officer. He held up a dynamo plant under Winfred's mattress. " Just as I suspected," said Professor Brown, gently picking up the dynamo from the officer's hands. " Now,Mr. Noble, if you do n't mind revealing your forepart." Winfred nervously brushed away some of his short crimpy hair to reveal, as suspected, a scar. A scar that both Andy and George had witnessed to seeing on the miscreant's forepart. The review said to look out for a man with green eyes, crimpy dark brown hair and a scar on his forepart.Mr. Noble had all of that, and indeed the black fleece, the muddy thrills, and a dynamo he tried to hide under his mattress. He'd committed the crime, and now he'd face the consequences. " No-I did n't-I would n't!" He contended. " Please! I did nothing wrong!"

Several officers dragged him down as he tried desperately to argue his innocence, but he was grasping at straws. Shortly after Winfred had been taken down, everyone had left the room. Everyone except for George, Andy, and the Professor. " You know, I had my dubieties about you, Professor," George said. " I did n't want to admit it. Now, however, you have easily proven yourself—you caught the Phantom of the Opera! Well done." George walked off to meet with the other officers, but Andy stayed before, saying he'd catch up latterly. " Is commodity bothering you, Andy?" Professor Brown asked. " Yes, there is." Andy looked up and made eye contact with the Professor, who was conforming his chapeau. " My mama lives in Pineville, and her birthday is, in fact, in October. I went to visit her on October 1st." Andy broke. "Mr. Brown, I've reason to believe that you're lying." Andy took a step forward. " Am I correct, Professor?" . Andy could see evil in his eyes.

He made a move to run, but it was too late.Mr. Brown took the dynamo that was plant under the mattress and fired, leaving Officer Smith lying on the ground. He put the gun on the ever still casket of the dead officer and took off his chapeau—revealing an oddly shaped scar on his forepart. He soughed.

" Well, that was dramatic."

SIX
RESOLUTION " 22

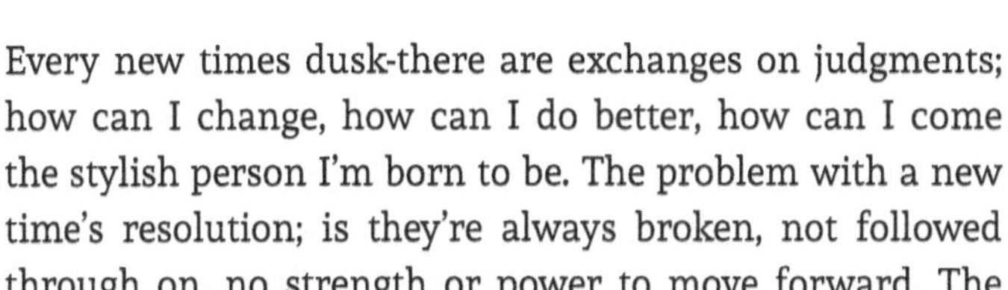

Every new times dusk-there are exchanges on judgments; how can I change, how can I do better, how can I come the stylish person I'm born to be. The problem with a new time's resolution; is they're always broken, not followed through on, no strength or power to move forward. The riddle of a resolution and why they've no backbone is because, there's no purpose.

It's just a game in society where people are pushed to suppose that their judgments will work. It's a fog like a cancer that is spread and blinds people from how to truly concentrate and push to gain their true capacities of seeing their worth in life. Resolution isn't what should be in our studies. The way to Approach a new time is learning how to truly push forward. To do so; with the Crucial word; Adaptability. Adaptability is defined in my eyes as; the power to jump over obstacles, overcome traumas with ease, to mime off the difficulties we run into; while pushing forward every waking moment. Being flexible means you believe in yourself; your tone worth, your mind and spirit.

Your body is a tabernacle and you must try to believe that you have the power to do anything.

Life has always been rocky from my perspective. Some people are Just dealt the bad hand in poker; but unfortunately you can not just fold When it comes to the' game of life'. There's a reason to be then; everyone was Born for a reason. Whatever that reason is; it means you have a purpose. Some People may noway know what their purpose is. But-with the power invested inside Of your soul; you can try to see what it is. It takes a true legionnaire to see the vision of themselves and Where they stand. If the vision is clear enough; adaptability could be attainable With ease. Occasionally however; there are outside factors that may block someone From their capability to achieve a resolution or come flexible. The words can be used interchangeably.

The words are just how You view it. I sat moment allowing what my purpose is. I've sunken myself into A pity of despair yet again. It's hard to dig yourself out of that hole. The Hole of darkness gets deeper and darker each time-the study of a resolution Or indeed a small step forward; or a more blunt way of putting it-the coming day seems Insolvable to manage. When life has been full of trauma, darkness, and in simpler terms just straight evil; while having relations with demons and the devil himself. It's hard to Do. So, if you were to see the side from someone in those shoes-how . Can you explain the purpose of life? What's the purpose of a new time's Resolution? What's the purpose of hereafter? What's the purpose of history? Are those questions that you can answer? Does the study of Those questions being asked; does it scarify you? Does the pure pain and immobility Of someone's life make you wonder? Is there similar thing of being flexible? Is It possible to move on from similar traumas; to come a stronger person? I've so numerous questions, without numerous answers. It's hard to Say or class those studies and I can slightly answer them myself.

It scares me to Suppose, another time coming? 2022? How will it dis out? Should I make judgments . Or should try to find adaptability. In a world so cold, dark and intimidating-is . It possible? How does one find the light when they're firmed in the history? Time. It moves slow, fast or the recollections stay on renewal. Now Being stuck in that revolving door of pain means the recollections, flashbacks and . Traumas stay on renewal. Any judgments you decide for yourself get pushed Away.

Because every day you fight demons, dark studies, the pain of wanting . It all to go down, the pain of being, the pain of wishing it noway happed, . The pain of wondering what it would be like if I was noway born. Those studies That are fought everyday takes the life out of you. It feels like this is not The life you should be living. Occasionally you get a boost and suppose to yourself-wow. Moment is A good day. Moment I can move forward and move on. But, lets pause and suppose to the future; the coming day you can not indeed get out of bed. The purpose of this short story is to tell a story about a fresh launch for someone that had a delicate time. When I started writing this story-I allowed to myself; wow I go I can suppose of a million ways how to tell a story like this. But-when I truly vision a new time's resolution or having adaptability in 2022-I can not indeed picture how to tell that story. All I've to say is; to suppose of where you started, what you have been through, how you made it out of those scripts and no matter where you may be moment-you can have a better hereafter.

Whether you're a freshman to a country, a woman escaping a poisonous vituperative relationship, a boy getting a man, someone that lost a friend or family member, a child in foster care, a person floundering with internal health-I want to believe that 2022 will be a good time. That this is the time that all of your judgments and dreams will come true within a certain time frame. Those scripts all feel like similar different aspects of life or different circumstances – but each bone has different hurdles to overcome. Each circumstance is given in life to certain people. Some people's lives may be easier; some people's lives are a lot harder. But; in reality-everyone has moments that test their capacities and help them grow and come flexible. Now I may be no award winning author or a pen, or indeed someone that went to academy for a field of this mastery; but these are my pure and utmost true studies.

My passions revealed on paper, no edits, no double thinking, just codifying aimlessly while feeling the worst I've felt in 27 times. So, I'm going to end this short story by saying; the grim reaper may control me and the devil may walk among us. But-with my adaptability and strength of a true legionnaire, my resolution will come my dream to succeed forth with. Moment I've the power to say yes, I can. Moment, I've the strength to have a better hereafter. My resolution is to move forward with strength of a bear, the knowledge of an owl, and the curiosity of a cat.

I drink 2022 with open arms and I wish anyone reading this-a time full of happiness, growth and spiritual removal. :)

A Special Note

To my amazing reading musketeers,

Huge, humble and sincere thanks to you for cheering me on through the hard corridor, encouraging me
to do my stylish at all times, making me laugh and feel connected to this community. And thank you for
buying **MIST OF MYSTRIES.**

It means the world to me that you would let my stories into your world.
It's all I 've ever wanted to do, as you can tell by these early scribblings.